Class No. ___J5-8___   Acc No. __C/252822__

Author: ___North, L___   Loc: __-5 NOV 2011__

LEABHARLANN
CHONDAE AN CHABHAIN

_____

_____

_____

1. **This book may be kept three weeks. It is to be returned on / before the last date stamped below.**
2. **A fine of 25c will be charged for every week or part of week a book is overdue.**   (Code 23)

0 8 MAR 2012		
2 4 MAY 2012		
0 8 JUN 2012		
0 2 FEB 2013		

D1433355

Jack
and the
Bean Pie

Bean Pies for sale

by Laura North and Mike Phillips

FRANKLIN WATTS
LONDON•SYDNEY

This story is based on the traditional fairy tale,
Jack and the Beanstalk, but with a new twist.
You can read the original story in
Hopscotch Fairy Tales. Can you
make up a new twist of your own?

First published in 2010 by
Franklin Watts
338 Euston Road
London
NW1 3BH

Franklin Watts Australia
Level 17/207 Kent Street
Sydney
NSW 2000

Text © Laura North 2010
Illustrations © Mike Phillips 2010

A CIP catalogue record for this book is available
from the British Library.

ISBN 978 1 4451 0176 7 (hbk)
ISBN 978 1 4451 0182 8 (pbk)

Series Editor: Melanie Palmer
Series Advisor: Catherine Glavina
Series Designer: Peter Scoulding

Printed in China

Franklin Watts is a division of
Hachette Children's Books,
an Hachette UK company
www.hachette.co.uk

For Christian – L.N.

Once, a boy called Jack lived in
a tiny house with his mother.

They had no money and just
ate vegetables from their garden.
But Jack was very good at cooking.
He made delicious bean pies.

One day, he took
the pies to the
market to sell.

6

"I'll buy your pies," said
an old man. "But I can only
pay with these magic beans."
Jack agreed and raced home.

Jack's mother was furious. "We need gold coins, not these useless beans!" she shouted.

She grabbed some beans and
threw them out of the window
in anger.

The next day, there was a huge
beanstalk in the garden. The
beans were magic after all!

"I wonder what's at the top?"
thought Jack. He started to climb,
up and up, into the clouds, until ...

… he found another world!
There were enormous flowers,
the size of trees. He saw a bee
the size of a horse!

13

Then a voice boomed,

"Fe fi fo fum ..."

"What's that?" thought Jack.

The voice got louder.

"Fe fi fo fum,
I smell the blood
of an Englishman!"

Suddenly, a huge hairy giant
stood in front of Jack.

He picked up Jack in one hand.

"Got you!" the giant growled.

Jack was terrified!

Jack had a few magic beans left in his pocket. He threw them at the giant and hoped they were still magic.

"Yum!" said the giant, "I love beans! They taste much better than humans."

Then the giant started to cry.
"I don't want to eat you at all,"
he sobbed. Big tears fell on Jack.
"The other giants make me
eat people. What can I do?"

Jack felt sorry for the giant.

"I've got an idea," he said.

"I can cook great pies. Let's tell the other giants they are human pies, but really fill them with beans!"

"Come and get your human pies!"
shouted Jack.

The hungry giants soon arrived.

As the giants gobbled up the pies,
Jack bravely jumped up.
"SURPRISE! The pies are full of
beans, not people!" he said.

"But this is the best pie I've ever had!" roared one giant.
"More bean pies!" they shouted.

The pies were so tasty that the giants forgot about eating people.

Soon Jack became rich and famous
from his bean pies. The giants
never tried to eat humans again.

Put these pictures in the correct order.
Which event do you think is most important?
Now try making up your own ending!

1. I'd like to buy your pies.

2. I have a very strong sense of smell.

3. I love cooking!

4. I wonder if the beans are magic?

5. I don't have any coins.

6. I don't like the taste of humans.

Choose the correct speech bubbles for each character. Can you think of any others? Turn over to find the answers.

Answers

Puzzle 1

The correct order is: 1e, 2f, 3a, 4b, 5d, 6c

Puzzle 2

Jack: 3, 4

The giant: 2, 6

The old man: 1, 5